To King, Shep, Jason, Tibbar, Schmitty, Wickett, Banjo, Jaeme, Chessie, Waddles, Utley, Quincy, Indy, and Suki – Thanks for letting me be a part of your lives. Best pets ever!

Chapter 1 – The Long Drive

Banjo lay curled in his favorite chair, licking his paws and waiting restlessly for his family to join him downstairs. He could hear barking from Roscoe, the Beagle next door, and knew that meant most of the neighbors were beginning their day. Although it was still early morning, Banjo was getting impatient because he and his family were going on a road trip to visit their Grandpa. Banjo knew this because he heard his family talking about the trip last night and it was mentioned that Banjo was going to be wonderful company for Grandpa.

Banjo was a little nervous about seeing Grandpa again because the last time they saw each other, Banjo had found some yarn on the guest bed where Grandpa slept and he had enjoyed chewing on the yarn and pulling and tugging at it until it finally was just one long piece of string. When Grandpa came into the room, he was very surprised and letdown to find that Banjo had just ruined his favorite sweater. Banjo tried to make it up to him later that day by sharing his favorite chair with Grandpa but when Banjo jumped in Grandpa's lap, he didn't notice the cup of coffee sitting on the table beside the chair, and Banjo's tail knocked the coffee to the floor. Banjo was afraid that Grandpa might not want him around anymore so he stayed in another room for the rest of that visit. Banjo had not seen Grandpa since and he sure hoped that Grandpa would not be disappointed to see him.

Banjo's family finally appeared for breakfast, and after eating pancakes and blueberries, they all loaded into the car with their luggage. Banjo was put in a crate to keep him safe on the drive and placed in the middle seat with his best friends, Lexi and Sami. Sami kept Banjo calm by sneaking treats to him, and they sang silly songs to him the whole way to Grandpa's house. Banjo was not afraid because he always felt safe when he was with his family. He was sure this was going to be a fun trip where they would all play together at Grandpa's house. It was a long drive though, and Banjo's stomach felt funny from eating all the treats. He decided to take a nap and slept for the rest of the drive. Banjo must have slept a long time because he had dreams of Grandpa and balls of yarn, treats, and even Roscoe, the Beagle.

Chapter 2 – Where Is Everyone Going?

Banjo heard car doors opening and suddenly everyone was climbing out of the car and hugging Grandpa in the driveway of his home. Lexi and Sami were showing Grandpa their new Taekwondo moves and were giggling uncontrollably as Grandpa tried to imitate them. He struggled to kick high over his head but his leg only came a little off the ground. When he tried to spin around, he fell on his bottom, chuckling with laughter, along with his family. Grandpa looked in the car and saw Banjo in his crate. He grasped the handle of the crate and carefully carried Banjo into his home. Grandpa then placed the crate on the floor and opened the small door so Banjo could come out. Banjo decided to remain where he was because he was still not feeling well from all the treats he ate on the drive. Grandpa fixed soup and sandwiches for everyone and then he heard Lexi and Sami's mom say it was time for them to be leaving. Banjo was confused because it seemed like they had just gotten there. Why were they leaving so soon?

Banjo slowly exited the crate so he could stretch a little before they took the long ride back home. Just as he started stretching, his family walked over to him and said they would see him soon. "Bye Banjo," said Sami. "Have fun with Grandpa." What was happening? Were they leaving him alone with Grandpa? "We'll be back before you know it," Lexi told Banjo. "Grandpa has been sad so try to cheer him up, okay?" Banjo knew that Grandpa had been lonely since Grandma had passed a couple of years ago. He could see pictures of Grandma all over the house and Banjo missed her too. She had been very kind when they were together and had given Banjo a toy mouse that squeaked when he pounced on it. She always seemed happy and she enjoyed playing games with Banjo. He could understand why Grandpa was sad but Banjo didn't know what he could do to cheer him up. He wasn't even sure if Grandpa wanted him in his home; but if his family wanted him to cheer up Grandpa, then Banjo knew he must try. Unfortunately, right after Banjo's family left, Banjo turned into Grandpa's kitchen and barfed all over the floor. "Oh no," Banjo thought. "This can't be happening again". Banjo recalled a time when a kind lady had taken him into her home when he was lost. He was scared and had gotten sick in her kitchen also. Now he had given Grandpa another reason to be disappointed in him. Banjo was sad because instead of comforting Grandpa, Grandpa was trying to make him feel better. "Don't worry little buddy," Grandpa said. "I understand you're nervous and you miss your family already." "I miss my Lovey too." Banjo remembered that Grandpa's name for Grandma was Lovey. Banjo and Grandpa both stared straight ahead in silence for several minutes. Finally, Grandpa picked up Banjo and carried him to his crate. Grandpa left the crate door open and told Banjo he could come out whenever he was ready. Banjo went back to sleep and had more dreams, but instead of treats and yarn and Roscoe, this time he dreamed of Grandpa and Grandma, and of ways that he could try to make Grandpa happy again.

Chapter 3 – A Walk in the Neighborhood

The next morning Banjo heard a dog barking and for a moment he thought he was listening to Roscoe waking up the neighborhood. But this dog had a different bark and Banjo began to wonder who this could be. Banjo didn't especially care for dogs, but this one sounded a little sad and Banjo hoped the canine was okay. Banjo thought maybe they could be friends.

When Grandpa came into the room Banjo crawled out of the crate and slowly walked over to him. Grandpa petted Banjo on the head and showed him where he had left some food and water. Banjo was feeling much better this morning and he was very hungry. He ate all of his kibbles and then followed Grandpa outside to his garage where he kept lots of old things that he had saved since he was a young man. Banjo especially liked the smell of the leather baseball gloves that Grandpa had made himself from his days working in a factory.

As Banjo continued sniffing everything he came upon, he noticed sitting by the garage door was a baby stroller. Banjo leaped up and sat in the stroller and this made Grandpa laugh. "How about I take you for a walk through the neighborhood little buddy?" Grandpa asked. "Imagine Ms. Audrey's face when she sees I'm pushing a cat instead of a baby," Grandpa giggled. Banjo liked that Grandpa seemed cheerful so he was all for this idea. Grandpa tucked Banjo in safely and off they went, strolling down the road.

Banjo was enjoying this walk because he could stay hidden if they came upon any dogs, and he could watch Grandpa as he waved to his neighbors. "Good Morning Richard," Grandpa yelled to the man on the ladder. Richard waved to Grandpa as he carried on with his chores. Banjo and Grandpa continued their walk until they circled all of Grandpa's street, greeting neighbors and delivery people along the way. Banjo even heard Grandpa laughing again as he watched children play hopscotch on the sidewalk. They had almost reached Grandpa's house when Banjo heard in the distance the sad barking from earlier this morning. Banjo peeked out from the stroller and saw a lady in the garden by her house. The lady turned and Grandpa waved to her. She carefully dropped the garden hose to the ground and came over to say hi to Grandpa. "What on earth do you have in this stroller," the lady asked Grandpa. "Well," Grandpa told her., "This little fella is called Banjo and he's staying with me for a while." The lady looked in the stroller and said, "You're a beautiful cat, Banjo. My name is Audrey and it's very nice to meet you." "Do you think Banjo would like to meet one of Casey's new puppies," Ms. Audrey asked Grandpa. "I think that would be okay," Grandpa replied. "I'll just push the stroller around to the side of the house and we can introduce them to each other," he continued. Banjo was getting a little nervous but he was also excited to meet the little puppy. Ms. Audrey left for a few moments and returned carrying a tiny little brown and white dog. "This is Suki, and she is the last one of the puppies that still needs a home,". Ms. Audrey told Grandpa that Suki was a Shih Tzu puppy, and her dog,

9

Casey, was Suki's mother. She said that Suki's brother was adopted earlier this morning and Casey was sad to see him go. Banjo realized that it must have been Casey barking this morning and now Banjo knew why she had sounded sad. Grandpa brought little Suki closer to Banjo and allowed them to play in the stroller for a few minutes. Banjo was happy once again to see the smile on Grandpa's face.

Grandpa and Banjo said good-bye to Ms. Audrey and Suki and they completed their walk to Grandpa's house. It had been a splendid morning and when Grandpa sat in his chair to rest for a while, Banjo jumped on his lap and cuddled next to him. Banjo felt that one good thing about Grandpa was that he liked taking naps almost as much as he did. They both nodded off and Banjo began dreaming again; this time about the nice lady Grandpa called Ms. Audrey, and a little Shih Tzu named Suki. Banjo didn't know it but Grandpa was dreaming the same thing.

Chapter 4 – The Old Record Player

Later that evening Grandpa fed Banjo his kibbles for dinner and the two of them sat together listening to Grandpa's music from the old record player. As soft music filled the house, Grandpa's joyful mood from earlier was no longer noticeable. Banjo watched as Grandpa gently picked up a picture of his Lovey and held it to his heart.

Banjo jumped from the comfy chair and walked over to Grandpa and meowed. Grandpa lifted Banjo, petted his fur, and kissed him on the top of his head. Banjo purred loudly and this made Grandpa grin again. "Banjo, what we need is some happy music," Grandpa exclaimed! Grandpa placed Banjo back in the chair and went to the record player. As pretty as the music was, Banjo could see that it was bringing up memories for Grandpa and making him sad. In a very short time, Grandpa had a new record on and this music was fast. Grandpa was singing along and he told Banjo that he and Grandma used to dance to this song. This didn't make Grandpa sad though. Instead, he was galloping around the room and he smiled at Banjo as he danced past him. Banjo had been worried that Grandpa wouldn't want him around, but he could now see that he was welcome in this home and he felt that Grandpa was actually enjoying his company.

Banjo and Grandpa listened to music all evening until finally, Grandpa told Banjo that it was time for bed. Grandpa said that tomorrow he would take Banjo on another walk in the stroller and this made Banjo happy. Banjo hoped they would visit the nice lady and her little puppy. When Grandpa got into bed, Banjo jumped onto the covers and curled up at the foot of the bed. As Banjo fell asleep, he wondered what Lexi and Sami were doing on their trip, and he hoped they were having as much fun as he and Grandpa were having.

Chapter 5 – Grandpa's Picnic

The next morning Grandpa and Banjo ate their breakfast while Grandpa read the newspaper. Banjo knew they were going for a walk and he was ready to get started, so he quickly gobbled up his food. Grandpa was eating too slowly for Banjo, so he hopped on

Grandpa's lap and began swatting at the newspaper. Finally, Grandpa gave in and cleaned up the dishes. He then went to his room and changed clothes, and then got the stroller from the garage and brought it into the kitchen. Banjo got comfortable in the seat and waited patiently while Grandpa packed a bag of goodies. Then, off they went down Grandpa's street. This time instead of circling the street, they turned at the corner. Banjo didn't know where they were going but he was sorry that he wouldn't get to see little Suki.

Just like the day before, Grandpa greeted the people he saw. It sure seemed like he knew everyone in town. He pushed the stroller into the Petway Animal Shop and bought Banjo a new squeaky toy mouse, just like the one Grandma had once given him. The man with the whiskers, who worked behind the counter, unwrapped the toy mouse and gave it to Banjo so he could play with it in the stroller. Grandpa also bought a leash and collar for Banjo so he wouldn't run off, but Banjo knew he would never do that. Remembering the time, not that long ago, when he had gotten lost in the city, Banjo snuggled into the stroller with his toy mouse. He was sure he would stay close to Grandpa so they wouldn't get separated.

When Banjo and Grandpa crossed the street, Banjo could see a park in the distance. Grandpa pushed the stroller to the park and stopped under the biggest tree Banjo had ever seen. Banjo thought the tree must have been very old because he could see that many people had carved their names and initials into its bark. As Banjo stared at the tree, Grandpa appeared with a blanket and spread it out on the ground. He then got out a little bowl of water for Banjo and lemonade for himself, along with snacks for both of them. He put the collar and leash on Banjo and attached it to the stroller, giving Banjo plenty of room to roam. Banjo had been on many picnics with his family and he wondered if they had told Grandpa how much he enjoyed them. The two of them sat under the tree for hours and Banjo even got to climb part of the tree before Grandpa brought him back to the blanket. Banjo was going to miss Grandpa when he returned home and he was sure Grandpa would miss him too. Banjo knew what he must do and he began making a plan. He just hoped Grandpa would go along with this plan of his.

     The two of them had a wonderful time at the park, and just when Banjo thought it couldn't get any better, Grandpa spotted an ice cream truck. "Banjo," Grandpa said, "It's a beautiful day for ice cream." Grandpa pushed the stroller over to the truck that read, 'Haley's Ice Cream'. A young woman who said her name was Haley asked what flavor Grandpa would like. He got a vanilla cone for himself and asked for a spoon so he could give Banjo a taste. Haley gave Grandpa a large vanilla cone and she put some ice cream in a spoon for Banjo and handed it to Grandpa. Grandpa thanked Haley and he and Banjo both savored their ice cream and then began their walk home.

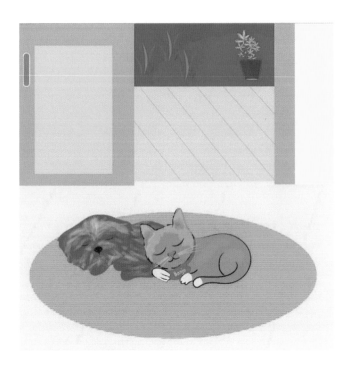

Chapter 6 - The Great Escape

When Banjo and Grandpa returned to his house the phone was ringing. Grandpa hurried in to answer it and Banjo could hear him talking on the speakerphone. Grandpa was talking to Lexi and Sami's dad and he told Grandpa they would be back to his house tomorrow to get Banjo. They had a fun time and were glad everything had gone well for Grandpa over the last couple of days. They were looking forward to getting home and to seeing Grandpa and Banjo.

Banjo heard the whole conversation and he was worried he wouldn't have time to put his plan into action. If his family would be at Grandpa's tomorrow, that meant Banjo only had a few hours and he needed to hurry.

Grandpa grabbed the bag he had taken to the park and put away the blanket and washed the cups. He gave Banjo some fresh water and took the stroller back to the garage. When he left the house, Grandpa must have thought he could trust Banjo because he didn't close the door. This gave Banjo the escape he needed to work on his plan. Banjo didn't like to worry people; especially Grandpa, but Banjo felt this was in Grandpa's best interest. He walked over to the door, looked both ways, and took off running. Banjo remembered his walk from the day before and knew exactly where he was going. He ran to Ms. Audrey's house and went around to the side of her home where she had introduced him to Suki. Banjo was confused when neither Ms. Audrey nor Suki was there. There was another dog that began barking and Banjo knew this had to be Suki's mom, Casey. The problem was Casey didn't know Banjo, so she barked and barked and had Banjo so scared he climbed behind some bushes so Casey couldn't get to him. Banjo didn't know it but Ms. Audrey was looking out the window wondering why Casey was so excited. She couldn't see Banjo and thought Casey must have seen a squirrel. Grandpa had started looking for Banjo but he was going down the street in the opposite direction. Banjo had heard that cats had nine lives and he was fairly certain that he had already used several of his. He hoped he would make it through this alive because even though Casey was not that big, she was clearly not happy that Banjo was in her yard.

Banjo stayed behind the bushes until it was almost dark. Casey was standing very close to Banjo with just a few branches between them, and she continued barking non-stop. Finally, Ms. Audrey came outside and Banjo could hear her trying to calm Casey. Banjo also heard a little puppy crying and thought that had to be Suki. Casey was suddenly more interested in Suki than Banjo so she quit barking. Ms. Audrey looked behind the bushes and saw Banjo's gray fur and white paws. She recognized Banjo immediately and called to him. When Banjo wouldn't move, she put Casey behind the gate so she could no longer get to Banjo. Banjo slowly came out from behind the bushes and Ms. Audrey carried him inside her house. Once Casey realized that Banjo was not a threat to her baby, she lost interest in Banjo and left him alone to play with

Suki. Ms. Audrey phoned Grandpa but he didn't answer because he was out searching for Banjo at the other end of the street.

After chasing a ball for a while, Suki and Banjo fell asleep on the soft carpet cuddled together. There was a knock at the door and Ms. Audrey opened it to a frantic-looking Grandpa. She led Grandpa into her house and explained how she had found Banjo and had tried to phone him to let him know that Banjo was safe. Grandpa was very relieved to see his little buddy and said he understood why Banjo had come to Ms. Audrey's house. They both could see that Banjo was very fond of Suki, but what they didn't realize was that Banjo could see that Grandpa and Ms. Audrey were very fond of each other.

Ms. Audrey made tea for Grandpa and they sat and talked until Grandpa said he'd better get Banjo back to his house because his family would be coming for him tomorrow. Grandpa told her how he had enjoyed Banjo's company so much and hated to see him leave. Ms. Audrey told Grandpa she was very worried because she still hadn't found a home for Suki, and having two dogs was too much for her. She wondered if Grandpa could help her find a suitable home for the puppy.

Grandpa didn't have to think too long about it and he told Ms. Audrey he knew just the person. He said he hadn't had a pet for many years and he would be grateful if she would let him adopt Suki. Having Banjo around these last couple of days had made Grandpa realize how lonely he had been and he felt Suki would be great company for him. Ms. Audrey was excited for Grandpa and Suki, and it was agreed that tomorrow Grandpa would return for Suki. Grandpa carried Banjo to his house and they headed for bed. As Banjo curled up at the foot of Grandpa's bed, Grandpa reached over and patted him on the head. "Thanks, little buddy. I have a feeling you had this planned all along." Banjo yawned, stretched and purred, and fell asleep.

Chapter 7 – Suki Moves In

The next day Banjo wasn't sure who was happier, Grandpa, or him. Banjo was thrilled to see his family, and when they arrived at Grandpa's house, Lexi and Sami smothered him with hugs and kisses. Grandpa told them all about their walks, the park, Banjo's escape to the neighbor's house, and finally, he told them he was adopting a puppy named Suki. Grandpa took his family over to meet Ms. Audrey and Suki and later they brought the little brown and white puppy back to Grandpa's house. Ms. Audrey had given Grandpa some food for Suki and instructions on training her. She was very happy that Suki would be living so close and hoped that she and Grandpa could take Suki and Casey for walks and let them play together. Grandpa thought this was a great idea and they made plans to meet the next day.

Before it was time to leave, Banjo jumped up one last time on Grandpa's lap. Grandpa rubbed Banjo's head and told him to come to visit him and Suki any time. He told Banjo the next time he visited he would take him back to Haley's Ice Cream Truck and they would let Suki have a little spoonful of ice cream. Grandpa said Banjo could have his very own cone because he was a special cat.

As Banjo and his family drove away from Grandpa and Suki, Banjo couldn't help but feel proud of himself. He was sure that Suki would do a fine job of cheering up Grandpa, just like he had done.

About the Author

Angela Mudrick is the author of the children's series, Banjo's Adventures. Other titles include Banjo's Adventure and Banjo's New Friend.